THE MYSTERY OF PELICAN COVE

Milly Howard

Bob Jones University Press, Greenville, South Carolina 29614

Library of Congress Cataloging-in-Publication Data:

Howard, Milly.
    The mystery of Pelican Cove / Milly Howard.
      p.   cm.
    Summary: Jimmy's sighting of a strange water creature gets the
community in an uproar, until its true nature is discovered.
    ISBN 0-89084-711-8
    [1. Sea monsters—Fiction.   2. Manatees—Fiction.   3. Christian
life—Fiction.]   I. Title.
PZ7.H83385My   1993
[Fic]—dc20   93-25966
                                                       CIP
                                                       AC

The Mystery of Pelican Cove

Edited by Karen Daniels
Cover art by Keith Neely
Interior art by Tim Davis

© 1993 Bob Jones University Press
Greenville, South Carolina 29614

ISBN 0-89084-711-8

15   14   13   12   11   10   9   8   7   6   5   4   3

To my husband Jack
for his support and encouragement

Books by Milly Howard

These Are My People
Brave the Wild Trail
Captive Treasure
The Treasure of Pelican Cove
The Runaway Princess
On Yonder Mountain
The Mystery of Pelican Cove

Contents

Chapter One
Strange and Salty Tales

" . . . and believe it or not, that sea creature led Blackjack right through the coral reef," Hiram said. The elderly caretaker's voice rose, and his eyes gleamed with excitement. He swayed back and forth as if the deck of Blackjack's ship shifted under his own feet. "Right past the Jaws of Death . . ."

"Sharks?" Jimmy squealed.

Hiram stopped to look at the three children sprawled at his feet. "No, the rocks that could rip a ship in half," he explained.

"Be quiet, Jimmy," whispered his brother, Paul. "Let Hiram finish the story."

"But . . ."

Paul's bony elbow in Jimmy's ribs cut off his sentence. Jimmy made a face at Paul, but he let Hiram continue his tale. "Out in deep water, Blackjack shouted for full sail. The *Jamaica Gull* sped away. The old men like to say that Blackjack leaned on the rail and shouted with laughter."

"He got away again," Elizabeth Anne said in delight. She jumped up and clapped her hands. Her sudden movement sent the bright red hair tumbling around her face. "How romantic!"

The two boys looked at their sister in disbelief. "Romantic?"

"Romantic!" Granny shook her head. "The man was a scoundrel, a thief, and a wicked pirate! Fancy tales don't make a fine man."

Hiram grinned cheerfully. "You can look that same story up in the library. The books will tell you exactly what I did. Blackjack was one of those privateers who attacked only enemy ships. A hero, he was.''

''Hero! Why, after the war, they almost hung him!'' Granny reached for the tray on the coffee table.

Jimmy hastily took the remaining cookies before the tray disappeared. He dodged as Paul tried to pry a chocolate chip cookie from his fist. Then he relented and gave Paul two of the cookies.

''Thanks, Jimmy,'' Paul said. He turned to Granny. ''But he did help, Gran,'' Paul said seriously. ''Blackjack kept enemy ships from landing on the coast.''

''Listen to him,'' Hiram said. ''If anyone knows the facts, it's Paul. You know we can hardly find him during the summer. If we really want him, we end up calling the library.''

''Everybody listen!'' Elizabeth Anne interrupted. She swung around and pointed to the open windows.

''What?'' Jimmy asked, scrambling to his feet. ''What?''

All five turned to look out the long windows. The ocean breeze stirred the lace curtains and rattled the shell chimes on the front porch. The porch swing creaked, and the palm leaves rustled. The only other sound was the waves slapping on the white sand below the house.

"Listen to the sound of the water," his sister said dreamily. "Just think; Blackjack could have dropped anchor right out there in our own bay!"

"I thought you heard a burglar," Jimmy said, losing interest.

Granny patted Elizabeth Anne on the shoulder. "We've certainly heard stranger tales," she said gently.

"I would have anchored in Pelican Cove if I had been Blackjack," Paul said thoughtfully. "A ship would be protected there."

"Yeah," Jimmy said, his interest revived. "He probably used our dock!"

"The dock wasn't here, silly," Paul said. "Blackjack sailed the seas in 1765. Didn't he, Hiram?"

Hiram nodded, heading for the kitchen. ''Right there abouts,'' he replied.

''What was it, Hiram?'' Jimmy asked. He hastily swallowed the last of his cookie crumbs and hurried after Hiram.

''What was what, Jimmy?''

''The sea monster that led Blackjack through the reef,'' Jimmy replied. ''What happened to it?''

''Well, it was a strange and wonderful—'' Hiram broke off as Granny gave him a warning look.

''There's trash to be emptied,'' she said.

''Well, I guess so,'' Hiram said with mock meekness.

''Go on with you, now,'' Granny said, laughing. ''And be sure to feed Blackie. I declare, that dog forgets I'm alive when Jimmy comes for the summer.''

Jimmy grinned. He liked the way Granny and the elderly caretaker teased each other, and he was used to what Granny called their "shenanigans." He returned to his questions, as persistent as Blackie going after a bone. "Really strange?"

"Well, it was no monster that I know of, Jimmy," Hiram continued. "A dolphin, maybe."

"Oh." Jimmy settled back down. "I saw one this afternoon. Out on the point. It was jumping."

"Probably a porpoise," Granny said firmly. "It's bedtime now. Upstairs with you."

"Aw, Gran," Jimmy said. "Can I help Hiram feed Blackie? I'm not sleepy."

"Tomorrow's another day, Jimmy, my boy," Hiram said. He pushed the kitchen door open and yawned widely. "How're you going to be of any use to me and Blackie in the morning? You need a good night's sleep just as much as I do. Up the stairs with you, and sleep tight."

"Goodnight, Hiram," the three children said, giggling. They headed for the stairs. Paul's long legs made him a sure winner, but freckle-faced

Jimmy was right behind him. Elizabeth Anne followed slowly, still wearing the dreamy expression on her face.

Granny hustled them along gently. "Pancakes for breakfast," she called.

Suddenly Elizabeth Anne came back to earth. "Making blueberry pancakes?"

"Come down and help mix," Granny said.

"See you first thing in the morning, Gran," Elizabeth Anne said.

"Elizabeth Anne's making breakfast? Ugh!" Jimmy exclaimed.

Granny laughed at the look on his freckled face. "She'll do just fine."

Paul looked down from the top of the stairs. "Watch out!" he called. "Elizabeth Anne has become an experimental cook. Cinnamon in broccoli; chili powder in asparagus. Takes some getting used to."

"Paul!" Elizabeth Anne's scowl wasn't pretend.

"Well, there had better not be chili powder in mine," Jimmy grumbled.

"Now, on to bed. We'll make the best blueberry pancakes ever!" Granny flapped her apron and shooed them upstairs.

Hiram stuck his head back around the door. He adjusted his old fishing hat on his white hair. "Going shelling in the morning," he reminded them. "If a body should want to tag along, he'd better be up before the crack of dawn."

"I'll be there," Jimmy promised. "Maybe I'll find something special."

Hiram's eyes widened in mock fear. "I hope not," he said quickly, closing the door behind him.

Jimmy grinned sheepishly. He had a habit of finding unusual things. More than once, his "finds" had caused trouble for the others.

"Just don't bring home anything that's dead," Paul called down. Once Jimmy had brought home a dead crab. It had taken them two days to locate the source of the smell.

"Or alive." Elizabeth Anne shuddered. Another time Jimmy had tried to make the tub into an aquarium for a baby octopus that he had lugged home in a pail. It had been days before Elizabeth Anne would even think about taking a bubble bath.

"Or valuable." Granny gave Jimmy a quick smile. Jimmy's liveliest adventure was the time he had brought home part of a buried treasure. Treasure hunters from up and down the coast of Florida had descended on them, watching Jimmy's every move. It had taken a full two weeks for things to settle back to normal.

Jimmy stopped on the last step. "I really can't bring anything home?"

Elizabeth Anne laughed at his woebegone look. "Okay, okay! Just keep whatever you find in your own bedroom, all right?"

Jimmy brightened. "You mean I can bring my stuff home? I can still keep it?"

"Of course, Jimmy," Granny said, her eyes twinkling. "Anything that won't fit on the plane to New Jersey can stay here at Land's End until next summer. Now up to bed with you."

Chapter Two
Trouble for Jimmy

The next morning the sun was glinting off the water before Jimmy awoke. The excitement and the long trip to the island had taken its toll, and he had overslept.

The buttery smell of pancakes sent him scurrying out of bed. He headed for the stairs. Elizabeth Anne stopped him before he slid down the bannister. She was standing at the bottom of the stairs, wiping her hands on a well-floured apron.

''Not in pj's, Jimmy. You know the rule.''

Now wide awake, Jimmy dashed back to his room to dress. He tugged shorts and a T-shirt from his suitcase and yanked them on. He almost beat Elizabeth Anne back to the kitchen.

He slid into his place with an eager glance at the screen door. "Yes! Yes!" he said. Blackie was there, nose to the screen.

Granny laughed. "All right. Let's say the blessing. I have a feeling that this boy won't take long to finish his breakfast."

Jimmy sighed with relief. Mealtimes were special to Granny, and she didn't like to see him rush through. But today was special too. This morning was the first day of the rest of the summer!

He managed to eat politely, even though his pancakes disappeared at an alarming rate. Then, with a milk mustache smile, he begged to be excused. A moment later, he and Blackie were on the path to the beach.

Both boy and dog headed toward the point where the cove met the ocean. A seagull swooped across the sunlit dunes. Blackie charged after it. Jimmy followed, plowing barefoot through the loose sand.

They spent the morning exploring the point. Then they headed toward the amusement park down below the restaurant. They were halfway down the beach when a shrill whistle rose above the sound of the surf. Blackie stopped short and pricked up his ears. Jimmy looked back at the wooden steps leading up to Granny's house. Hiram was standing on the bottom step holding a net of shells. He yelled something, but the wind caught his words and whipped them away. Jimmy waved, and Hiram pointed toward the house. He must be going in.

Jimmy waved again. As Hiram started up the path, Jimmy climbed back toward the road. Blackie lumbered out of Jimmy's way and rushed up the slope. He reached the road and began to bark. Jimmy struggled up after him.

"Move over, Blackie," he said. "Let me see."

Blackie thrust his nose into a patch of dried grass that grew along the road. The grass quivered as the dog nudged at his prey.

Jimmy parted the wiry strands. A soft-shelled turtle lay upside down on the ground. "A gopher," Jimmy said. "You got a big one this time, Blackie."

He picked the turtle up and ran his fingers around the flat rim. "Turtle, if Granny gets hold of you, you'll be soup for sure."

Blackie followed Jimmy across the road. The boy put the turtle down under a palmetto. Then he squatted beside his dog. They watched the turtle, but it made no effort to come out of its shell.

Jimmy wiped his face with his sleeve. His movement caused a ripple across a palmetto leaf. Jimmy inspected the leaf curiously. Another ripple of light and shadow crossed the leaf. The leaf rattled dryly. Quickly, Jimmy scooped his hand across the quivering leaf. He closed it over a wiggling lizard.

"A lizard! Look, Blackie!" He opened his hand just enough for the dog to get a glimpse of the lizard's head. "We can keep this one."

Blackie barked.

"Hey!"

Jimmy looked back at the road. He had been so busy with the lizard that he hadn't heard the bikes approaching. Four boys had stopped and were watching him. He tucked the lizard into a pocket of his camp shorts and zipped it in. "Come on, Blackie," he said. "Let's go!"

He backed out from under the palmetto. He and Blackie trotted across the road. The boys were waiting for him.

"What do you want?" Jimmy asked. One of the boys seemed to be the leader of the group. Jimmy looked at him expectantly.

"Whatcha got?" the boy said.

"Hey, Buck," one of the boys interrupted. "It's one of the kids who stay with Mrs. Thompson every summer. You know, in that big old house called the Landing."

"Land's End," Jimmy corrected.

"Got that, Buck?" The boy grinned.

The boy called Buck didn't answer. He was still eyeing Jimmy's pocket. "What did you find?"

"A camellon," Jimmy said, putting a protective hand on his pocket. The lizard squirmed.

Buck laughed. "A chameleon," he corrected Jimmy. "And it didn't look like one to me. How about you, Ken?"

"Nah. Just a green lizard."

"It is too," Jimmy said defiantly. "I found it and it—it was changing colors just like the books say it does."

"Hey, aren't you the kid that found the emerald last year?" Ken asked.

"Pegleg's treasure?" Jimmy's eyes brightened. "Sure."

"Aw, come on," the boy scoffed. "Nobody found any treasure. They just tore up the beach for nothing."

"I bet there wasn't an emerald at all." Buck gave Jimmy a sly look. "Just one of old Hiram's crazy tales."

Jimmy glared indignantly. "Hiram's not crazy!"

"He sure talks a lot." Buck shrugged. He looked at Jimmy's pocket again. "Let's see the lizard."

Jimmy unzipped his pocket and fished out the lizard. He held it up. It wiggled and shot out of his fist. It landed on Buck's shirt and leaped back across Jimmy's shoulder. Another leap took it to the grass on the other side of the road. It was gone before Jimmy could move.

Buck hooted. "Some chameleon. A little green lizard! You must take after your Hiram, for sure! Jewels and lizards!"

Jimmy felt his face begin to burn under his freckles. "You take that back!"

"Look at that temper!"

"Wanta fight, kid?"

"You wouldn't dare say that if my brother was here!" Jimmy shouted.

"How old is your brother, kid?" Buck grinned. "No, let me guess. He's probably nine, right? Too little to mess with."

"Paul's ten! And he's big enough to take care of you!"

"Come on, Buck," one of the boys complained. "We were supposed to be at Eddie's an hour ago."

Buck leaned on his handle bars. "Tell that brother of yours I'll be waiting," he said with a mock shudder.

The boys rode away, still laughing. Jimmy stood in the road glaring after them. And all he could do was clench his empty hands.

Chapter Three
A Shape in the Dark

Jimmy didn't say much on the way home. Blackie seemed to sense his change in mood. The dog trotted along beside Jimmy, panting quietly. Jimmy was still frowning when he reached Land's End.

Hiram was watering the hibiscus hedge that curved from the side of the house down towards the water. He turned off the spray as Jimmy charged past.

"What's wrong, Jimmy?" he asked.

"I lost my camellon," he said.

"Camellia?" Hiram sounded puzzled.

"No, my lizard."

"Sorry," Hiram said. "Bet it was a big one, huh?"

Jimmy nodded. Hiram always made him feel better. "It barely fit in my pocket! It was a good one!"

"It's the big ones that always get away," Hiram said. "Never you mind, you'll find it again some day. Or Blackie will. Hey, did I ever tell you about the time a little green lizard saved Old Maloney's life?"

"No," Jimmy replied, rolling up the garden hose for the caretaker. "What happened?"

He followed Hiram about the yard, helping with the yardwork as the old man told his tale. "I guess that was the great-granddaddy of my lizard, wasn't it, Hiram?"

"Well, maybe . . ."

The dinner bell rang. Hiram had hung the old farm bell next to the kitchen door so Gran wouldn't have to chase them down when it was time to eat. Jimmy's stomach rumbled. He forgot about everything that didn't look, feel, or smell like food.

After lunch, Hiram settled down for his nap. Jimmy went back to look for his lizard. He didn't see it, though he and Blackie looked long and hard.

Jimmy finally gave up and went to look for Paul. His brother was sprawled across his bed reading a book.

"Play with me?" Jimmy said hopefully.

"Uh," Paul grunted.

Jimmy didn't even try again. It was impossible to get Paul out of a book once he passed the first chapter. Instead, he picked up a book of his own and wandered downstairs. Blackie met him at the screen door. He wagged his tail.

"Not now, Blackie," Jimmy said. "It's too hot."

Blackie whined. Jimmy opened the door and went out on the porch. He found a wicker couch in a shady corner and curled up. Blackie lay down beside him. Jimmy read until Granny started working in the kitchen. The smell of chocolate drew him inside.

"Can I help?" he asked, eyeing the bowl of chocolate icing.

Granny laughed and handed him a spoon. Jimmy's favorite rule at Land's End was the one Granny repeated. "If you frost the cake, you get to lick the bowl. But don't eat too much. You'll spoil your supper."

She didn't say it too firmly, though. Jimmy never had trouble eating at Gran's house. He thought Granny's cooking was even better than Mom's.

After supper, he and Paul cleared the table. Elizabeth Anne and Granny washed up while Hiram got out the big Bible. They gathered around the table as he read from James 3. *"Even so the tongue is a little member, and boasteth great things. Behold, how great a matter a little fire kindleth!''*

Jimmy's heart sank. He knew those verses by heart. He'd heard them often enough at home. Jimmy avoided Elizabeth Anne's meaningful look. Avoiding Paul was harder. He was sitting right across from him.

Jimmy looked down at his hands, remembering that boy, Buck. He had an uneasy feeling that he had almost committed Paul to a fight. And Paul wouldn't like that at all. He listened half-heartedly to the rest of the passage.

I do try, he thought miserably, but somehow the words just jump out when I get mad.

Almost as if he'd read Jimmy's mind, Hiram said, ''You know, it's pretty hard, sometimes, to keep our tongues from getting us in trouble, but that's something God can help us with. Now let's pray.''

Jimmy hardly heard Hiram's prayer. He was thinking about Buck and doing some hard praying of his own. He didn't want Paul to get in trouble because of something he had done.

That night, Jimmy read his nature magazines until Paul finally insisted that he turn off the light. Then Jimmy lay awake, staring around the moon-lit room. He almost told Paul about the boys, but he decided to wait for God to answer his prayer.

Still, he couldn't go to sleep. He listened to the waves lap at the shore below the house. He listened to Paul's deep breathing from the other bed. Jimmy turned over to watch his brother sleep. But another sleeping person only made him feel more wide awake.

Jimmy threw back the covers and moved quietly over to the window. He pushed the window up as far as it would go. Then he leaned on the sill and looked out. The waves surged gently. Nothing else moved on the shining surface of the water. He stayed by the window for what seemed a long time. His eyelids began to droop. Suddenly a shadow crossed the sand below the window.

Jimmy blinked and focused on the shadow. It moved steadily up the path to the house. Jimmy's heart raced and his eyes widened. Then the shadow stopped. It seemed to look back at the dock. In the pale light, the shadowy profile of a dog showed clearly. Jimmy let out his breath in a muffled laugh.

"Blackie!" he whispered. "Making his rounds!"

Jimmy left the room, moving quietly on his bare feet. Downstairs, he padded through the hall to the kitchen. When he unlocked the door, Blackie was there, wagging his tail.

"Hi, Blackie," Jimmy whispered. "No burglars here, huh?"

Blackie wagged his tail harder and tried to lick Jimmy's face. Jimmy hugged him. "Didn't see any dolphins or whales out there, did you?" he asked.

The dog gave him another nudge. Jimmy laughed. "I see you didn't. Come on, I'll go with you."

Blackie led Jimmy around the side of the house. The boy waited patiently as Blackie sniffed around a flower bed. Then the two moved toward the back of the house. They crossed the wide yard and went toward the boathouse.

Blackie trotted down the length of the wooden dock and peered into the water. Jimmy followed and sat on the edge of the dock. He rolled up his pajama legs and dangled his feet in the water. Blackie stretched out beside him and watched Jimmy's feet churn the water.

In the distance, lights rimmed the far edge of Pelican Cove. The lights sparkled like tiny fallen stars. Sometimes a starlike light floated somewhere between land or sky. The floating lights were boats anchored in the bay. Pinpoints of light clustered in sweeping arcs that followed the shoreline.

"See the brightest patch of light over there, Blackie?" he asked. "That's the cannery where the fishermen take their catch."

He and Blackie watched the bobbing lights on the bay. Jimmy squinted his eyes a little. He could just make out the shadows of the boats under the

running lights. Jimmy's eyes focused on a darker shape. At first he thought it was the shadow of a boat too. Then it moved. Jimmy stared, wondering why a boat would be under way without running lights. Blackie stiffened beside him.

A cloud crossed the moon and darkened the sky. When moonlight again lit the water, there was nothing to be seen. No shadow, no shape, nothing. Jimmy relaxed, and Blackie lay back down again.

''Must have been that cloud, Blackie. It probably made the shadows seem to move.''

Jimmy's feet again splashed back and forth in the water as he talked to Blackie. He yawned. He was thinking about going inside when the dark shadow appeared on the water again. It was closer, much closer.

Blackie was on his feet before Jimmy could swallow the lump in his throat. The dog quivered as if he were straining to see. Jimmy widened his eyes, trying to get a clearer view of the shape. It sank slowly into the water.

"A submarine?" Jimmy asked in amazement. "Why would a submarine be here?"

Blackie stood watching the spot where the shadow had disappeared. Jimmy stared at the same spot. The dark shape surfaced again. Now it was only fifty yards away. Both boy and dog shrank back.

The shape surged forward, rolled, and curved toward the dock. Jimmy yanked his feet from the water.

"It's alive!" he gasped.

Blackie whined as Jimmy scrambled backwards on the dock, then he barked twice and bolted after Jimmy. The two reached the kitchen door at the same time. Jimmy leaned against the door to catch his breath. He looked back at the water.

The thing rolled away from the dock and disappeared. It broke water about twenty yards out. Then it disappeared again.

Jimmy forced himself to take one breath at a time. When his heart slowed its leaping, he said out loud. "It's gone, Blackie." The dog shrank against the boy's legs. When Jimmy opened the door, Blackie whined and looked up at the boy.

"Okay, boy," Jimmy whispered. "Okay. You can sleep with me tonight. Just be quiet."

He and Blackie crept upstairs. Once safely in bed, Jimmy pulled the covers over his head. He wasn't going to move for the rest of the night.

Chapter Four
Jimmy's Monster

"Wake up, Jimmy!"

Jimmy rolled over, groaning in his sleep. The sheet tangled around him. He thrashed back and forth, trying to escape.

"Let me go! Let go!" he yelled.

"Hey, Jimmy!" Paul shook him again. "Wake up!"

Jimmy opened his eyes reluctantly. Paul sat on the edge of the bed, watching him. Jimmy struggled with the coils of his sheet. Paul found one corner. He jerked it, bouncing Jimmy around as he unwound the sheet.

"Boy, you must have had a rough night," Paul said. "What's going on?"

Jimmy sat up and tried to smooth down his hair. "Nothing," he answered. "Why?"

"You were moaning in your sleep last night," Paul replied. "Something about a monster."

Jimmy looked around for Blackie. The dog was gone.

"I let him out," Paul said. "Early this morning. The kitchen door was unlocked."

Jimmy rubbed his face, trying to think.

"Don't bother," Paul said. "I can see the wheels trying to turn. You can't tell me Blackie unlocked the door and came in himself. Therefore, somebody had to let him in. It wouldn't be Gran or Elizabeth Anne, and it wasn't me. So that leaves you."

"I couldn't sleep last night," Jimmy confessed. "I saw Blackie making his rounds, so I went down."

"You went outside at night?"

"It was as light as day," Jimmy said.

"So what happened?" Paul asked.

"What makes you think anything happened?" Jimmy said uneasily.

"You don't talk in your sleep every night," Paul said. "Usually you sleep like a log. And you didn't get up to go shelling with Hiram. So what gives, Jimmy? Come on, let's hear it."

Jimmy hesitated. His fear of the moving shape dissolved in the bright sunlight that streamed across the room. "You'll laugh."

"No, I won't." Paul sounded positive.

Jimmy took a deep breath. "I went out to sit on the dock with Blackie and we saw a monster in the water and it came right at us and we ran."

Paul grinned. "A monster?"

"You promised not to laugh!" Jimmy was indignant. He bounced out of bed and reached for his clothes.

"Settle down, Jimmy. I'm not laughing."
Paul got up. "Come on, show me where you
saw it."

Jimmy dressed quickly and followed Paul to
the kitchen. His sneakers squeaked on the tiled
floor as he stopped abruptly. One place was set at
the table with a bowl for cereal and a glass for
milk. Jimmy's stomach gurgled.

"Where's Gran?" he asked.

"She and Elizabeth Anne went shopping,"
Paul said, grinning. "Since you were sleeping so
late, I got left behind to take care of you. You
saved me from a fate worse than death. Thanks,
pal."

"Cost you fifty cents." Jimmy's voice was
hopeful.

"No way. I'm saving my money to get that
Skyhawk model I saw at Herlich's, back home. I
found out that Capt'n Hawkins will pay for minnows. He sells them for bait."

"Can I help?" Jimmy asked.

"Maybe," Paul replied.

"We can split the money fifty-fifty."

"Twenty-eighty," Paul offered.

"Forty-sixty?" Jimmy gave him a pleading look.

"Thirty-seventy," Paul said firmly. "Take it or leave it."

"I'll take it," Jimmy said. "Come on."

The two walked out on the dock. Jimmy sat down with his cereal. "Out there," he said, waving his spoon toward the bay.

"What did it look like?"

Jimmy finished his first spoonful of cereal before answering. "About three times as long as you, I guess. It was big. I thought it was a submarine at first."

"So what changed your mind?" Paul scanned the water.

"It turned and came toward us, I told you," Jimmy said impatiently. "A sub wouldn't do that."

"Moonlight plays tricks on you," Paul said. "You probably saw a log moving with the current."

"Upstream?" Jimmy said in disbelief. He hadn't spent his summers on the water for nothing.

"Well, maybe it was a boat," Paul said. "Maybe the skipper saw you. Maybe he decided to see who was on Gran's dock in the middle of the night. Or maybe it was one of Hiram's dolphins."

Jimmy's spoon stopped midway to his lips. He put it back down and stared blankly at the water.

"Well?"

"I don't know," Jimmy replied. "Maybe."

"Well, finish up and ride down to the fish camp with me," Paul said. "We'll look for clues on the way."

The road to the fish camp ran right along the river. The boys biked slowly, looking for anything unusual. But there was nothing different about the crushed shells that spun under their wheels. Nor was there anything unusual about the water that lapped around the river weeds. Out on the bay, boats moved back and forth on the water. Seagulls circled lazily around the barges, and pelicans sat motionless on the channel markers. By the time they reached the fish camp, even Jimmy was beginning to think his monster was a dream.

Captain Hawkins was cleaning out bait boxes. He hosed down the last one and began filling it with sea water.

"Hi, boys," he called. "Ready to work? The net's over there. I'm getting low on bait."

Jimmy gathered up his end, careful not to drag the net over the rough boards. He and Paul made their way along the bank.

"This looks good," Jimmy said.

"Well, I guess we can try here," Paul said. "I'd rather go farther up."

"We'll have to drag the net back," Jimmy complained.

"Oh, all right. But fan it out so we can cover as much water as possible."

Jimmy walked the net out until he was chest high in the water. He refused to go any farther. "I fell in a hole once," he said. "And once was enough."

"You can swim like a fish," Paul replied.

"Yeah. But that hole stunk."

"Bet you're still worried about your monster," Paul teased.

"What monster?" The question came from above them.

Jimmy looked up at the bank and groaned. Neither Paul nor Jimmy had heard Buck and his friends approach. But there they were, balancing their bikes on the sandy bank and grinning.

Jimmy was beginning to think that the boys were trying to sneak up on them. It was pretty hard not to hear bikes, especially on a dirt road. He glanced at Paul. His brother gave the boys a friendly smile. Jimmy's heart sank. What if Paul

got in trouble? He had to get rid of the boys before Buck remembered everything he had said about Paul.

"Was it green?" Buck asked, grinning.

Jimmy frowned. "No, it wasn't," he snapped.

Paul looked at him in astonishment. Jimmy looked away.

"Touchy-y-y!" One of Buck's friends drew the word out into a siren sound.

"How big was it? This big?" Buck held his hands six inches apart. He and his friends howled with laughter. "Did you tell Hiram?"

Jimmy's eyes blazed. "It was three times as long as . . . as . . . as Paul here! And it charged right at me! It opened its jaws and I thought it was going to rip the dock apart!"

"It attacked you?" Buck bent double with laughter. "What did you do? Grab a harpoon and bring it down?"

"Hey, boys! That's enough!" Captain

Hawkins's voice boomed across the water. "Move on, now."

Buck and his friends obeyed, still laughing. Jimmy watched them ride back toward town. Slowly he turned to face Paul. His brother was still staring at him, open-mouthed.

"What was that all about?" Paul asked.

Jimmy's heart felt heavy enough to be used as an anchor. He faced Paul and tried to shrug. He hadn't meant to add all that extra about the monster. "They were teasing me yesterday. About Hiram, the emerald, and everything."

"Why didn't you say something?"

Jimmy pulled at the net. "Granny says we don't have to settle everything that happens. God will take care of it," he said defensively. He thought about his prayer. At least Buck hadn't said anything to Paul.

"Granny also says not to add fuel to a fire," Paul replied.

"What?"

"Not to keep something going by making it worse," Paul explained. "Didn't you hear what Hiram read last night about the tongue being like a fire? Whatever made you tell them it attacked you?"

"Did it?" Captain Hawkins stood above them. "Did something attack you?"

"Aw, Capt'n," Jimmy replied. "I went out on the dock at night. There was just something in the water—"

"And you ran?" the captain asked.

"I ran." Jimmy confessed. "Blackie ran too."

"Good move." Captain Hawkins grinned. "I'd run too, if I saw something big in the dark. Tell you what. I'll keep a lookout for anything unusual. If I see anything, I'll let you know."

"Thanks, Capt'n," Jimmy said, cheerful again.

The two boys pulled the net in. They emptied their catch into the boxes. Then Jimmy stowed the net while the captain paid Paul. They got their bikes and pedaled up onto the river road, squishing water from their sneakers with every turn of the pedals.

"Hey, boys!" the captain called after them. "I got two charters tomorrow. Come early, and I'll pay you double!"

"Sure thing, Capt'n," Paul called back. He surged ahead of Jimmy. "Race you, Jimmy!"

Chapter Five
Disaster at Pelican Cove

Jimmy didn't forget about his monster. There was no way he could if he wanted to. Everybody on the island had heard about it by the end of the week. When he went into town with Granny, even the bag boy at McBride's Groceries knew.

"Hey, are you the guy that saw the monster?" A grin threatened to split the boy's face into two rubbery halves.

Jimmy ducked his head.

"Maybe we got our own Nessie," the boy teased. "Right in Pelican Cove. Pelican Cove Nessie!"

"That's enough, Jefferson Courtney Templeton," Granny said quietly. "Jimmy just told what he thought he saw."

"Jeff, ma'am. Just Jeff." The boy looked around quickly as if he were worried that someone had heard his full name. He hastily filled the last bag and offered to carry the bags to the car.

"Thank you, Jefferson, but Jimmy likes to roll the cart. We'll take care of the bags. See you at church Sunday."

Jeff winced. "Sure thing, Mrs. Thompson." He lowered his voice. "Remember, it's Jeff."

"Of course, Jeff," Granny said gently.

That stopped the discussion, but it didn't end there. On the way to the parking lot, a reporter from the *Pelican Cove News* hailed them. "Are you the boy who saw—"

"Yes," Jimmy said. "And I wish I had never gone outside that night!"

"That bad, huh?" The reporter reached for a pencil. "Good thing for us that you did. News has been so slow that I've been thinking about rerunning the old legends about pirates. This monster tale will liven sales up even better."

"Liven sales?" Granny's eyebrows went up.

"Sure, ma'am," the young man said cheerfully. "Folks want to read about more interesting things than when the Garden Club meets. And this is about the most interesting news we've had in months. Now, son, how big was this monster?"

Jimmy sighed. "About three times as long as Paul."

"Who's Paul?"

"My big brother," Jimmy replied patiently.

"And it attacked you?"

Jimmy squirmed. "Well, no, not exactly."

"Oh, but I heard that it charged the dock where you were sitting." The young man's bristly mustache quivered. "That's just the spice that this story needs."

"Well, it came toward the dock, but not—"

"Fine, Jimmy. That's fine. Now what did it look like?"

"Uh, just a shape . . ."

"Flat head? Any humps?"

"Uh, I—"

"Excuse us," Granny said firmly. "It's time to go."

"Well, could it have had humps, son?" The reporter wrote quickly.

"I guess so," Jimmy said. The stream of questions confused him. Hastily, he got into the car and slammed the door. Granny drove out of the parking lot and turned toward the fish camp to pick up Paul.

"I've never been so embarrassed in my life," Elizabeth Anne said. She put her hands in front of her face as they passed the gas station.

"Don't fret, child," Granny said. "Like the reporter said, there hasn't been much excitement on the island lately. Folks will settle down when nothing else happens.''

''You don't believe me?'' Jimmy said in a small voice.

''Why, Jimmy,'' Granny said kindly. ''I think you saw something. You know how things look bigger than they really are in the dark. Maybe it was a bottle-nosed dolphin.''

Jimmy sighed. He knew it wasn't a dolphin. He thought about the big surge of water he'd seen as whatever-it-had-been swam toward the dock. No, it hadn't been a dolphin.

He didn't leave Land's End all that week. He even let Elizabeth Anne bring books home from the library for him. The teasing had taken its toll. He didn't want to run into Buck and his bunch. And the last thing he wanted was to see the monster again.

Jimmy spent the next few days out on the point with Hiram. Life settled down to the normal summer routine. His collection of shells grew. He even found one conch that Hiram said was the best he had ever seen. Whatever he did, he kept a good distance from the dock at Pelican Cove.

The teasing died down, just as Granny said it would. Then, one foggy morning, he and Paul arrived at the fish camp for another morning of catching minnows. They found a group of excited fishermen crowded around Captain Hawkins.

"Ripped into toothpicks," said one ruddy-faced tourist. "Sent the *Boston Lady* drifting out to sea. I got up early to fix the coffee. I stepped outside to check the mooring line. I looked up and saw a freighter bearing down on us. I tell you, the coffee went one way and I went the other!"

"Didn't you hear anything in the night?" A puzzled islander scratched his head. "I've heard of sound sleepers, bud. You must take the cake."

Jimmy gave Paul a puzzled look.

"That means he's hard to wake up," Paul whispered.

"We'd come in from a day trip to the reef," the man explained. "My wife and I were dead tired. The whole dock could have gone and I wouldn't have heard it.''

"It did," the captain said dryly. "Whatever hit your floating dock broke its mooring and set it adrift. And it's a good thing you docked the *Boston Lady* near the end. Otherwise, you'd surely have heard something!''

Jimmy edged closer. "What happened?" he asked.

The captain looked at Jimmy and chuckled. "Well, son," he said. "I promised to let you know if anything unusual happened. Guess this is the right time. Your monster crashed into the pilings over in Pelican Cove. Took off one floating dock and set this man's boat adrift.''

Jimmy stared. "My monster?''

"Anything big enough to do that deserves to be called a monster," the tourist said. "What was it? A whale?''

"I've heard of whales coming in," the captain said. "They usually run aground though. Anybody sight one?''

The fishermen shook their heads. "One ran aground on Shell Beach last winter. That's all."

"Did you say the boy saw this thing?" The tourist shoved his way through the crowd. "What was it like, boy?"

Jimmy took a deep breath. "Big."

"How big?" The man was impatient.

Jimmy backed away nervously. "About three times as long as Paul here," he said quietly.

The man whistled. "Fifteen feet?"

"I guess."

The crowd murmured in excitement. Jimmy got the net and tried to pull Paul away. Finally Paul followed him. When they had filled the bait box, Jimmy was ready to go.

"Okay," Paul said. "You go on. I want to stay a while."

Jimmy shrugged. He took the change Paul gave him and headed home. This time he went straight to the back and parked his bike by the kitchen door. Then he whistled for Blackie. Even

with the dog at his side, he approached the dock
cautiously.

He and Blackie waited for nearly an hour.
Jimmy lay down on his stomach and rested his
head on his arms. He watched every ripple on the
water. There was nothing to show that anything
big lurked in its depths. Only an occasional mullet
broke the surface. Blackie chased seagulls off the
dock as if he had forgotten about the monster.
Jimmy finally gave up.

"There's nothing here now," he said to
Blackie. "But there was. I just know it. I'm tired
of people thinking I'm silly. I'm going to find out
exactly what I saw!"

Chapter Six
Running Scared

The next morning Hiram brought the newspaper up to the house. "Just look at this," he chuckled. "Pelican Cove's Nessie has hit the headlines again."

"Jimmy!" Elizabeth Anne wailed.

"Not me," Jimmy said, wiping milk off his upper lip. "I had nothing to do with it."

"Something destroyed a dock yesterday," Paul said. "What does it say, Hiram? Do they know what it is?"

Hiram read the article aloud. It was full of speculations and hints about strange underwater creatures. No real evidence was given to explain what had happened to the dock. Jimmy's sighting was compared to the Loch Ness monster.

Granny shook her head. "That young reporter is pushing the facts just a little too far."

"Well, that happens, you know," Hiram said, folding the paper. "Folks are always trying to prove that something like the Loch Ness monster exists. Livens up life somewhat."

"Like your stories?" Granny's question sounded innocent.

Hiram frowned. "My stories are true. Well, mostly."

Usually Jimmy liked to hear them tease each other, but today he just wanted to get away by himself.

"May I be excused, Gran?" he asked.

"Of course," Granny said. "You too, Paul and Elizabeth Anne."

Jimmy hurried outside, feeling guilty. He wished he had never said anything about the thing attacking him. He wished he could take the words back—just erase them like erasing words from paper.

Blackie trotted out of the shade. Jimmy rubbed the dog's head. "Hiram was right about the tongue being like a fire. I feel like I started a fire that I can't put out!" Silently he made an addition to his prayer about Buck. Please Lord, he prayed, help me not to make up stuff, not even when I'm mad.

He looked down at Blackie. "Maybe I should keep my mouth shut all the time!"

Blackie wagged his tail.

"I guess not," Jimmy said. "Then who'd talk to you, huh?"

He and Blackie walked down to the dock. Jimmy lay face down on the warm boards. He peered between the boards and listened to the lazy slapping of water against the pilings. The water was deeper than it looked. Long ago Hiram had dredged the river bottom near the bank. He had wanted to bring a big boat into the boathouse.

Jimmy knew it was plenty deep. He, Paul, and Elizabeth Anne had dived off the end of the dock often enough. Close to ten feet. Deep enough for something big to get close to the dock. But not deep enough for anything to come close without being noticed.

Jimmy wished that he hadn't run away. The creature couldn't have come out of the water any-way. His fear of the monster had gone. Granny's calm suggestions had sent monsters back to the land of make-believe.

Jimmy couldn't lie out on the dock all morn-ing. He went back to the house. Elizabeth Anne was gathering books to return to the library. He asked to ride with her.

"I want to get some more books," he told her.

"I'm in a hurry," Elizabeth Anne said. She gathered up her fine hair in a ponytail. It promptly broke loose and curled in wisps around her face. "Oooh! Why couldn't I have had hair like yours!"

"Mine?" Jimmy asked, puzzled.

"Yes, it's blonde and straight," Elizabeth Anne moaned. "Why did I get stuck with carrot hair?"

She pulled out some of Granny's crinkle hairpins and stabbed them around her hairline.

"I bet Granny's hair was just like yours before she turned gray," Jimmy said. "I think it's pretty."

"Hmm." Elizabeth Anne turned back and forth in front of the mirror. "You really think so? I look like Gran?"

"Yeah. Can I go with you?"

"Okay. Get your books then. Just mind your manners. And NO talking about monsters!"

"I promise," Jimmy said. "And I can ride back with Paul. He's at the fish camp."

"Check with Gran, then." Elizabeth Anne admired her ponytail in the hall mirror. "I'm ready to go."

When Jimmy got back, Elizabeth Anne had forgotten the ponytail and was popping bubble gum in front of the mirror.

"It's going to end up stuck to your face," Jimmy warned.

"It's old, anyway," Elizabeth Anne said, dumping the gum into the trash. "Miss Abbott won't let anybody into the library with chewing gum."

Jimmy got his bike and waited for Elizabeth Anne. She put half the books in his basket, and they started off.

"Come on, Blackie," Jimmy called.

"Can't that dog stay home once in a while?" Elizabeth Anne asked. "He's getting too old for all the running around you two do."

Jimmy looked from her to Blackie. The dog wagged his tail and whined. He sat down beside Jimmy's bike and barked.

"Oh, all right," Elizabeth Anne said. "Nobody would recognize you without that dog anyway."

"Thanks," Jimmy said.

Elizabeth Anne didn't answer, but she rode more slowly than usual. Blackie trotted next to Jimmy's bike. When they reached the library, Blackie lay down outside.

Miss Abbott smiled when they came in. "Back so soon?"

"Yes, ma'am," Elizabeth Anne replied. "I finished these. Now I'm looking for a mystery by Anne Whitton."

"You know where to find it, don't you, Elizabeth Anne?" Miss Abbott stamped a book for an elderly lady. "What about you, Jimmy?"

"I'm looking for a book about Nessie."

"Nessie? . . . Oh, you mean the Loch Ness monster."

Jimmy nodded. Elizabeth Anne gave him an irritated look and moved away.

"You'll find some picture books in the animal corner. Over where the chairs are. And I'll see what else I can find for you."

Jimmy was glad that Miss Abbott hadn't laughed. Maybe she hadn't heard about his monster. He headed straight for the animal corner. He found a book about whales and paged through it until Miss Abbott handed him several more books. "Thanks!"

"Happy hunting," she said with a smile.

Just as he'd hoped, she had given him a book about the Loch Ness monster. He spread it open on a table and scanned the pictures carefully. They left him more puzzled than before.

The thing he had seen didn't look a bit like the drawings and photos of Nessie. He opened some other books on undersea creatures and studied the pictures in them. Nothing seemed to fit.

He was looking at a book about sea mammals when Elizabeth Anne finished. "Hey," she said. "It's three-thirty. Gran will be wondering what happened to us."

"Look at this," Jimmy said. He held out the book. "Look at the babies."

Elizabeth Anne leaned over to see. "Uh-huh. Why don't you check it out? We're running late."

"Okay," Jimmy replied. He added the book to the stack he had already chosen.

They took the books to the desk in the front room. Elizabeth Anne handed Granny's card to Miss Abbott.

"Seen anything more of your midnight visitor, Jimmy?" the librarian asked.

Jimmy shook his head and reached for his books. She leaned over and spoke to him quietly. "I heard the boys talking. Don't let them get to you," she said, tucking a pencil over her ear. "They like to give summer people a hard time— just teasing, you know. They'll get over it."

"Hiram's not a summer person," Jimmy said.

"Hiram can take care of himself," Miss Abbott replied. "He's quite a character, that man. Some people don't understand characters."

"Characters?"

Miss Abbott thought for a moment. "Special people."

"Yes, ma'am." Jimmy didn't see, but he didn't ask again.

Blackie rose as they came out the door. He waited while they loaded their bikes. Then he led the way down the road. When they reached Captain Hawkins's baithouse, Jimmy waved good-by to Elizabeth Anne.

"See you at supper," she called back.

Jimmy found Paul leaning against a refrigerated box, drinking a Coke.

"Can I have one?" Jimmy asked.

Paul reached inside and pulled out a Dr. Pepper for Jimmy.

"I'd rather have a Yoohoo," Jimmy protested.

"You and your chocolate," Paul said. He fished in the icy water and brought out a chocolate drink. "Here."

"Thanks," Jimmy said. He looked from Paul to the men gathered around Captain Hawkins. "What's going on?"

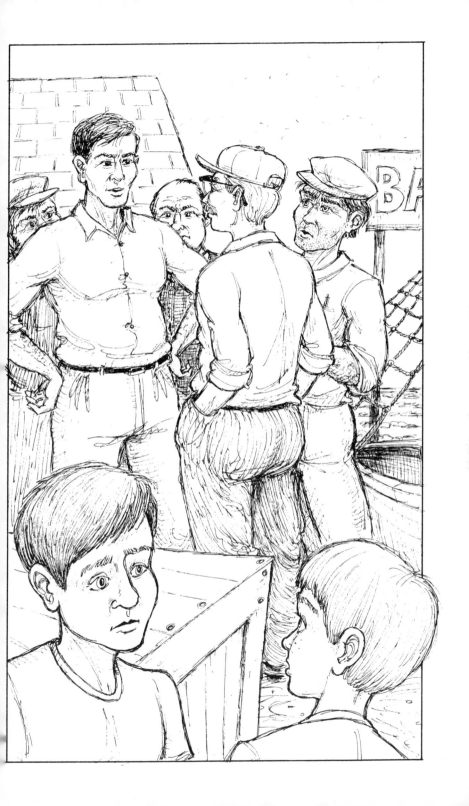

"They're fishermen," Paul explained. "Something ripped their net and they lost a big haul of fish. They're pretty mad."

"Who's that big guy?" Jimmy whispered. He nodded toward a tall, thickset man in the middle of the group.

Hands on his hips, frowning slightly, the man seemed to be in control of the group. He asked the fishermen questions in a quick, sharp tone. They answered him angrily.

"Who is he?" Jimmy repeated.

"Oh, sorry," Paul replied. "I was trying to hear what he's saying. He's the owner of the cannery on the mainland. Across the bay."

"What's he talking about the monster for?"

"He doesn't believe in monsters," Paul said. "He says it's just a large sea animal and it can be taken care of just like any other pest."

"Pest?" Jimmy was horrified.

"The *Margaret Belle* is down until the nets are mended. The cannery needs the fish. The owner doesn't want to take any chances of losing more equipment or any more time. He's telling them—''

''—I can hear,'' Jimmy said. ''He's telling them to shoot it!''

Chapter Seven
A Chance Meeting

Jimmy found Hiram in the back yard. He swung himself up on a low-hanging limb of an orange tree. He watched the caretaker trim the trailing branches of a climbing rose. Hiram whistled as he snipped the overgrown branches and clipped the others back onto the trellis.

"You're looking a mite glum today," he told Jimmy. "Where's the boy who used to come knocking on my door at five in the morning? I've had the beach all to myself these last few days."

"I've been staying up late," Jimmy confessed. "I saw the sea creature first at night. I thought it might come back."

"You're slipping out of the house after we are asleep?" Hiram frowned.

"Blackie is with me," Jimmy replied hastily. "Anyway, there's nothing moving that time of night."

"I don't like it," Hiram muttered. "Fishermen carrying high-powered rifles, a sea creature loose in the bay, and you out on that dock in the middle of the night."

"Blackie lets me know if anything is coming. Then we lie flat on the dock."

"So what have you seen?"

"Mostly trawlers, fishing boats. They're running more lights than they used to. And every boat has a guard posted with a rifle. They're going to *hurt* it." Jimmy gave Hiram a pleading look. "Can't you do something?"

"You come and get me, son," Hiram said. "I'm a mite slow at waking up in the middle of the night. But if that's what it takes, I'm game."

"Game?"

"Ready for action. We'll both find out what kind of creature is disturbing the bay," Hiram explained.

Jimmy's face brightened. "Thanks, Hiram!"

"No problem." Hiram was clipping at a stubborn branch. "As long as I don't doze off the next day. I'd hate to clip my toes off."

"I'll keep you awake," Jimmy promised.

Hiram groaned. "All right. But we have to tell your granny."

Jimmy frowned. "She might not let me."

"Better to tell the truth now than be sorry later. Remember, *he that speaketh lies shall not escape.* Go on, now. I'll put in a good word for you," Hiram told him.

Jimmy agreed reluctantly. Gran and Hiram always insisted on the truth. So did his parents. He went to the kitchen to find his grandmother. She wasn't there, and he didn't search for her. He went back outside. "I'll tell her tonight," he thought. "After supper."

He got his fishing pole from the boathouse and went out on the dock. He had two mangrove snappers in his pail before Blackie started barking. Jimmy peered into the water. Nothing moved under the dark surface. He hushed Blackie and prepared to cast again.

Footsteps on the dock startled him. He looked back to see Paul striding toward him. "Catch any fish?"

Jimmy shook his head. "Just turtles." A movement in the reeds along the bank caught his attention. He let the rod fall to the dock.

"Fine with me," Paul said. "If I never see another fish, I'd be happy."

"Shh!" Jimmy leaned forward. He waited breathlessly for another movement. He was beginning to think that a sea breeze had ruffled the reeds when a surge of water hit the dock. Under the surface he glimpsed a dark shape like the one he had seen before.

"Whoa!" Paul jumped back.

"Be still," Jimmy pleaded.

A whiskered head surfaced just out from the dock. The creature lay back in the water, using flippers to hold something small to its chest. Jimmy stared. He had seen a picture of something doing just that. He just couldn't remember what it was.

"What is it?" he whispered.

Paul stared at the creature. "It's a sea cow, I think. A manatee."

"A sea cow," Jimmy whispered to Blackie. "It's a sea cow, and a baby."

He lay on the dock watching the monster that wasn't a monster feed its young. The two rolled over in the water and plunged back toward the grass. The manatee was about fifteen feet long, as Jimmy had guessed.

She seemed unaware of the boys' presence. She turned toward the water plants and sank out of sight. Jimmy's mind raced. He couldn't remember much he had read about the sea cow, just bits and pieces. She was only a huge shadow under the water, but the baby rolled about in the reeds. Jimmy held Blackie to keep him from leaping at it. The dog's barking brought the mother back up.

When the sea cow led her baby into the inlet near the dock, Jimmy got his bright idea. The inlet was a dead end. He had seen Hiram barricade the inlet to block a run of mullet. The sea cow had to come back the same way she came in. "Hey, Paul," he said. "Let's block her in."

"What on earth for?" Paul asked. "She's fine where she is."

"But they're hunting her," Jimmy said. "All we have to do is keep her here, and she'll be safe."

"Well," Paul said thoughtfully, "Mr. Flint over at the cannery is offering a reward for the creature—or monster as the fishermen call it."

"A reward?" Jimmy asked. "What would he do that for?"

"She's interfering with fishing," Paul said. "We should call the game warden."

"What would he do with her?" Jimmy asked.

"Don't ask me," Paul replied. "He'd see that she was taken care of, I'm sure."

' "Well, I'm doing it." Jimmy set his jaw. "She's my monster."

Paul laughed. "No! Look what Jimmy brought home this time! Just wait until we try to get it on the airplane!"

Jimmy waited until Paul stopped laughing. "It's still mine," he said. "Can't we help her?"

"Yeah, I guess so," Paul said. "We can try using Hiram's burlap, but I don't think it'll hold her."

"Okay!"

Jimmy padded barefoot along the dock to the boathouse. He found a long roll of burlap that Hiram had weighted along one end. Paul helped roll it out. They scooted it along the dock. Then Paul unrolled it and let the cloth slide slowly into the water. He and Jimmy jumped in and dragged the cloth over the water to the mouth of the small inlet.

The burlap looked like it was more than twenty feet long. It took Jimmy and Paul the better part of an hour to get it across the mouth of the inlet. Paul clipped the hooks on the edges of the cloth to the metal loops Hiram had driven into posts on either side of the inlet. Then he swam back to the dock and inspected their work.

Gravity and the current worked together to slowly pull the billows out of the burlap. Jimmy didn't know how long it would take for the burlap to settle. He hoped it would be in place before the sea cow wanted to get out.

"Paul," he said, watching his brother climb back onto the dock.

"What now?" Paul said, grinning.

"Promise not to tell."

"No way." Paul shook his head. "You can't keep her locked up in there forever."

"Just one day," Jimmy pleaded. "Then we can get all this settled down. She'll be safe until we explain to the men what she is."

Paul thought a moment. "All right. One day. That's all. But if anyone asks me about her, I'm not lying."

"Thanks, Paul," Jimmy said.

Paul chuckled. "This has to be the strangest thing you ever brought home!"

Jimmy followed his still laughing brother to the kitchen. Paul's laughter disappeared as he sniffed the air. "Blackberry! The only pie better'n blueberry is blackberry!"

"It's for supper," Granny warned. She took the blackberry pie out of the oven and put it carefully on a hot pad.

"When's supper?" Jimmy asked.

"In good time."

"Guess what I heard, Granny?" Paul said, pulling out a chair.

"Now what have those men been up to?" she asked.

"How do you know it's the men?" Paul asked.

"You've been at the fish camp, haven't you?" Granny's smile made her eyes twinkle.

Before Paul could answer, Hiram came through the door holding the evening paper. "Listen to this." He read the headline aloud. *"Flint Offers $1,000 for Monster!"* He shook his head. "Every man and child who can hold a gun will be combing these waters for Jimmy's monster. That crazy galoot says he wants the creature dead."

"Why?" Elizabeth Anne asked. "Why not just capture it?"

"He's a big-time business man," Hiram said, "and he's got no time to waste on some poor water animal. At least not if it's causing him problems."

"How can it cause so much trouble?" Jimmy asked. "It just broke a net and banged into a dock."

Granny put on her reading glasses and picked up the paper. "Seems like it's more than that, Jimmy," she said slowly. "It has broken several nets. And last night it overturned a small fishing boat.''

Hiram snorted. ''They probably ran over a submerged log. And nets break for other reasons. I'm beginning to think Jimmy's sea creature is being blamed for more than its share of damage.''

''Perhaps,'' Granny said. ''Island folk tend to be a bit superstitious. They've gotten all worked up, and they're not thinking straight. Jimmy, I don't want you out at night any more. Not until this is settled.''

Jimmy looked at her in surprise. ''You *knew?*''

''I know every creak of this old house,'' she said tartly. ''And those I've heard lately weren't house sounds. Now, no slipping out at night, young man.''

''Yes'm,'' Jimmy said weakly.

Paul gave him a strange look.

Jimmy opened his mouth to tell them about the sea cow, then he shut it. After all, his mouth was always getting him into trouble. Why not hold his tongue a bit, he thought. At least until he knew what was going to happen to the sea cow.

Chapter Eight
In Hiding

Jimmy had planned to visit the sea cow after everyone had gone to sleep. Granny's warning had changed his plans. He thought again about telling her, then hesitated. He thought the sea cow was probably safest where she was. He wanted time to find out more about her.

He went to bed with his books. Paul finally put the covers over his head to block out the light and went to sleep. Jimmy found the sea cow in the book about sea mammals. He read the short section over and over. When he finally put the book down, he knew only a little more than before. He knew that this sea cow was big, as sea cows go. He knew that they fed on water plants around the shore. He knew that the baby would stay with its mother until it was two years old. That was all. He made up his mind to go to the library again the next day—after he had told Granny about the sea cow and her baby.

The next morning as he walked into the kitchen, he wondered how to tell Granny and the others. Before he could speak, Hiram came through the back door. He shook his head in disgust.

"They're out in full force," he said.

"In force?" Jimmy's heart leaped.

"Lots of them. Twenty boats must've passed in the last thirty minutes. An easy thousand is more attractive than a hard day's work." Hiram looked disgusted.

"Just as it has been from the beginning of time," Gran added. "So are the ways of everyone that is greedy of gain."

Elizabeth Anne spread butter neatly into the four corners of her toast. "Well, I think they are awful, even if the thing is a monster."

Jimmy slid into the seat opposite Elizabeth Anne. He took a big swallow of milk. "It isn't a monster," he said finally. "Gran, it's a sea cow."

"A manatee?" Hiram's shaggy eyebrows rose.

Granny put down the coffee pot and looked at Jimmy. "And how do you know, Jimmy?" she asked.

"I saw her yesterday," he confessed, "when I was fishing off the dock. She has a little baby."

"Why didn't you say something, Jimmy?" Granny asked. "You could have stopped all this nonsense about killing. Manatees are protected by law."

"They are?" Jimmy's voice squeaked with excitement.

"That's why I said to get the game warden," Paul said. "You hardly see them anymore. People used to hunt them for their hides and oil. That's why they are so scarce."

"But the folk around here ought to know that a manatee isn't a monster," Hiram protested. "What's wrong with them?"

"They got stirred up by a simple mistake made by a boy whose story was stretched—"

Jimmy flinched, but Granny went on.

"By a young newspaper reporter who wanted 'news' rather than facts. The result is being used by a strong-minded man who is using other people to get his own way."

"And now what will they do when we tell them it's a manatee?" Elizabeth Anne asked.

"I'm not sure," Granny said. "But the truth is always better than a lie, spoken or unspoken." Then she quoted, "*The lip of truth shall be established forever: but a lying tongue is but for a moment.* That's Proverbs 12:19."

"You are absolutely right. We'll make a trip into town this morning." Hiram said firmly. "I've had a hankering to speak to Mr. Flint for the last few days."

"Can we go check on the manatee first?" Jimmy asked.

"How would we find it? The hunters haven't," Elizabeth Anne said reasonably.

"It's in the inlet," Jimmy said. "We put Hiram's burlap across the mouth to keep it in."

"We?" Granny looked at Hiram.

"Not Hiram. Paul," Jimmy said.

When Granny turned to Paul, he looked embarrassed. "Well, it was—it was the thought of Jimmy bringing in one of his finds."

"If you don't beat all," Hiram began, his eyes twinkling. "That one would be hard to fit on a plane!"

Then his face went still. "You put it in the inlet by the dock?"

"Yes, sir," Jimmy replied. "What's wrong, Hiram?"

"Nothing, probably." Hiram sounded uneasy. "The weights aren't heavy enough to keep that burlap down when the tide comes in and out. Maybe the manatee got past it—''

"No!" Jimmy groaned.

He shoved his chair back and ran. Hiram grabbed his hat and beat the others out the door. They reached the inlet just as Jimmy stumbled into the water.

"The burlap's up," he yelled. "I bet she got out!"

He half-swam, half-splashed up the inlet with Elizabeth Anne and Paul behind him. Granny and Hiram followed them. "No, she didn't! She's here," Jimmy called back. He struggled toward a dark mound in the water.

"Oh, my; she got beached at low tide," Granny said. "Don't get too close, children. Wait!"

But Jimmy had already reached the manatee. The baby squealed and rolled toward its mother. The big sea cow twisted frantically, but she couldn't move.

"Easy now, Jimmy," Hiram said. He moved up behind Jimmy and raised his hand to quiet the splashing of the others. He touched the manatee gently. "It's already getting dry."

Jimmy gave him a stricken look. "I thought I was protecting her," he said tearfully.

"You were," Granny said. "You probably saved her life last night, but this morning she has a different problem. She needs help, Jimmy."

"What can we do?" Jimmy asked. "What?"

"You and Paul go unhook that burlap and drag it up here," Hiram said. "The first thing we need to do is protect her from the sun—maybe with the burlap. Then we need to keep her wet until the tide changes."

"Come, Elizabeth Anne," Granny said. "There are some buckets up on the back porch. We'll need enough for all of us."

Jimmy and Paul struggled around the bend, pulling the weighted burlap through the water. Hiram splashed back to them and took one end.

"How did you ever get this across the inlet, Jimmy?" Hiram asked. "It weighs a ton."

Jimmy resisted the impulse to make up something really heroic. "We floated it on the water," he said. "It was dry and it took a while to sink."

"Then let's get the water to help now," Hiram suggested. "Pull the end with the weights and let the other end float."

They dumped the burlap near the manatee. Jimmy and Paul began straightening out the billowing folds. "We need something to keep it up," Hiram said. He cut some branches from the bank and pushed them into the sandy bottom of the inlet in an arc away from the sun. Then they wound dried vines around the branches to keep them from sliding.

The manatee seemed to settle down and resign herself to the people moving around her. The baby manatee kept close to its mother, making whimpering sounds. When Elizabeth Anne poured the first bucket of water over its mother, the baby squealed. The mother reached for it with a flipper, and it shrank back against her.

Granny talked in a soothing voice to the sea creatures as she and Elizabeth Anne poured

bucket after bucket of water over them. The manatee turned, revealing a deep scar along her back.

"What's that, Hiram?" Elizabeth Anne asked. She touched the scar tissue.

"Looks like she got hit by a propeller some time ago," Hiram said. "People don't see them and ride right over them in the water."

"Don't you have enough branches yet?" Jimmy asked anxiously. "It's getting hotter."

"That burlap's wet, and it's heavy," Hiram reminded him. "We've got to make sure the branches will support it."

When he was satisfied, he cut the weights off the burlap to lighten it. Then the five of them raised it over the lattice of limbs. When they finished, the branches sagged under the weight.

"Will they hold it?" Paul asked doubtfully.

"Well, the cloth won't get any wetter. As a matter of fact, the sun'll dry it out," Hiram said. "It'll get lighter and those limber branches will straighten right out."

They had positioned the burlap to block the morning sun that blazed over the shimmering water. Still, it took all five of them working constantly to keep the manatee soaking wet.

Finally Jimmy put his bucket down. ''Is she going to make it?'' he asked shakily.

Hiram and Granny looked at each other. Granny put her arm around the boy. ''The water's rising, Jimmy. Feel it? It won't be long until she's free.''

''But will she be all right?'' Jimmy looked at the manatee. Now it lay listlessly in the water.

''Only the Lord knows how she'll respond to being out of water,'' Hiram said. ''But she wasn't in the sun long, and we've kept her wet. She should be all right.''

''I hope so. I sure hope so. And Gran,—'' Jimmy said fervently, ''I'll never hide anything from you again!''

Chapter Nine
The Secret Is Out

The water deepened around the sea cow. The tired rescuers stumbled to the bank to rest. The baby was playing freely now. It swam in and out of the tangle of mangrove roots and canes that hid the inlet from the river. Suddenly it surfaced near the bank and squealed.

"He's stuck," Jimmy said in alarm.

The baby had wiggled into a cavelike tangle of roots and couldn't find its way back out. Its squeals sent its mother into a frenzy of motion. The powerful thrusts of her body swirled clouds of sand through the water.

"Hey, she's going to hurt herself," Paul exclaimed. "Get that baby out of there!"

Jimmy and Elizabeth Anne swam over to the roots and shooed the baby back the way he had come. Once her baby was free, the manatee calmed down.

"That's what happened to the nets and the dock," Granny said. "She has an adventurous baby to look after. I reckon she's had to charge into some pretty tight places to rescue that curious little one."

Hiram chuckled. "Reminds me of someone we know, doesn't it?"

"The baby?" Elizabeth Anne said. She grinned and everyone looked at Jimmy.

"Me?" Jimmy was astonished.

"No, of course not you," Elizabeth Anne said. "Just who else do you think gets into all the trouble around here?"

Jimmy gave her a sheepish look and turned back to the manatee. "Hey, she's covered with water now. Look at her!"

The manatee gave a sudden lurch and sent water surging up the bank. She rolled and was free. Jimmy watched in amazement as she nudged her baby toward the mouth of the inlet. Before they could move, she was gone.

They sat on the bank for a few minutes, looking at the burlap flapping in the breeze. Finally Hiram moved. "I reckon I'd better take it down."

"What'll happen to the manatee?" Jimmy asked. "Couldn't we have kept her here?"

"No," Granny said gently. "We just didn't have a good place to keep her. She needs deep water. But—"

She clapped one hand to her head.

"What is it, Gran?" Elizabeth Anne said, alarmed.

"I should have called the game warden before we rushed down here," she said. "He ought to know what to do about her."

"He certainly ought to put a stop to this hunt," Hiram said. "They can't kill a manatee

—at least, not in these waters.''

''Let's go phone him, Gran,'' Elizabeth Anne said. ''Hurry!''

''I'm in no shape to hurry right now, child,'' Granny said wearily. ''But I'm coming.''

At the house they waited as she placed the call. The game warden wasn't in. Granny left a message on his answering machine.

''Well,'' she said firmly as she hung up. ''There's one person I know who's in!''

''Who?''

''Mr. Flint.''

Granny dialed the number of the cannery. She made an appointment to see Mr. Flint that afternoon. When she hung up, Jimmy gave a sigh of relief.

''Thanks, Gran,'' he said. He wrapped his arms around her in a bear hug. ''I really made a mess out of things.''

''It's not over yet, Jimmy,'' she said. ''Getting something like this straightened out isn't like sewing up a torn shirt. But, yes, we'll do our best to see that your manatee isn't hurt.''

''Can we go too?'' Paul asked.

Granny hesitated. ''It wouldn't hurt Mr. Flint to see that even children are concerned about the manatee. But you must promise to be courteous and not interrupt.''

''We promise,'' the three children promised. ''Thanks, Gran!''

Granny looked at Hiram. He lifted his shaggy eyebrows innocently.

''Well,'' she said, smiling, ''I suppose you have your speech all ready. Get your hat, then.''

Hiram grinned and pulled his hat from behind his back. ''Yes, ma'am.''

Granny shook her head. ''You're just like the children. No, you're worse. You ought to know better.''

''Yes, ma'am.'' Hiram winked at Jimmy. He clapped the hat on his head.

Granny began to laugh. "We're a sorry looking crew," she said. "I don't think we'd impress anyone like this. Up the stairs with you, children, and put on your Sunday best. We're going to beard the lion in his den!"

"Beard the lion?" Jimmy looked at Gran.

"Talk to Mr. Flint face to face," Elizabeth Anne explained cheerfully. "And we all get to go!"

An hour later, Hiram got the car out of the garage. The children settled in the back. Jimmy felt as if he were on the way to church. Hiram drove, and Granny sat up front with him. All five were quiet on the way across the bridge to the mainland.

Finally Jimmy broke the silence. "Do you think he will listen to us, Gran?"

"I don't know, Jimmy," Gran said. She gave him a smile. "We'll do the best we can. Then we must leave the matter in the Lord's hands."

"No better place, Jimmy," Hiram said gruffly. "If he knows the sparrow . . ."

"Then he knows all about the manatee," Paul said. "Relax, Jimmy."

Jimmy wasn't sure. He knew God's power. He knew God answered prayer. Hadn't He kept Buck from fighting Paul? But this whole problem was his fault. And he had a feeling that it would get worse before it got better.

He was the last one out of the car at the cannery. Trucks roared past them, noisily shifting gears as they swung around to the loading dock. When Hiram opened the doors, the clatter of machinery made Jimmy cover his ears. It didn't seem as if the cannery was slowing down at all.

"Up here." Hiram motioned above the din.

They followed him up a flight of metal stairs. He opened a door on the landing and ushered them in. The door swung shut, cutting the noise off abruptly.

They were standing in a carpeted, panelled office. Across the floor was a well-polished desk. At the desk sat Mr. Flint's secretary. She stopped typing and gave them a surprised look.

"We called about the manatee," Hiram said. "I guess you could call us a delegation."

"Yes, sir." The secretary pushed a button on the intercom. "Mr. Flint? Mrs. Thompson and . . . the family are here to see you."

"Send them in," barked a voice.

"Thank you," Granny said to the secretary as they went in.

Jimmy stayed as close to Hiram as he could without actually touching him. Across the room, a big desk took most of the space in front of a bank of windows that opened onto the cannery floor. Jimmy could see machinery moving and people shouting as they loaded boxes. Without the noise, they looked like puppets. Inside the office there was silence.

A man rose from the desk. "What can I do for you?" he asked, looking at his watch.

"We won't take much of your time, Mr. Flint," Hiram said. "So let me get right to the subject. It's about the reward you put out for the sea creature."

Mr. Flint motioned to the chairs in front of the desk. Granny sat down gracefully, and Hiram took the other seat. The children stood behind the chairs. Mr. Flint sat back down and placed his fingers together, watching them curiously. "You want the reward?"

"Heaven forbid," Granny replied. "This creature that has stirred up so much fear is only a manatee—a sea cow."

Mr. Flint's face was unreadable. "So?"

"A manatee is protected by law, Mr. Flint," Hiram said. "I'm sure you are aware of that. You must remove this reward and notify the papers to make sure that no one kills this animal by mistake."

Mr. Flint rubbed his chin. "Didn't the creature damage the nets and the dock?"

"I suppose so," Granny said. "She has a small baby. It could have been part of the reason the damage was done."

"Well," Mr. Flint said suddenly, standing up. "I'll tell you what I'll do. The reward stands.

Manatee or not, it's delaying shipments and de-creasing our supply of fresh fish. I'll notify the paper to change the offer to capture only. Thank you for bringing this to my attention, Mrs. Thompson. My secretary will see you out.''

Outside, Jimmy looked at Hiram. ''Will the manatee be safe now?''

Hiram put a hand on Jimmy's shoulder. ''I don't know, Jimmy. I don't think we made much progress.''

Granny smoothed her gloves thoughtfully. She and Hiram looked at each other. Finally Granny said, ''I agree. As long as Mr. Flint sees the man-atee as a threat to his profits, it isn't truly safe. What that manatee really needs is a home. And perhaps we can get it one!''

Chapter Ten
Speaking Out

Jimmy stepped back into the shade of a store awning and put his hands into his pockets. He stared across at the newspaper office.

"Gran," he said suddenly.

Granny didn't hear. She was talking to Paul.

"Gran!" Jimmy said loudly.

The others turned to look at him.

"What if we talk to the newspaper reporter?" he asked. "You know, that guy who asked me so many questions?"

Granny looked at him with respect. "The newspaper! Yes, Jimmy, that's exactly what we should do. But first, we need to arm ourselves."

"Arm?" Jimmy was puzzled. "With guns?"

"With facts." Granny straightened her hat. "Elizabeth Anne, let's visit Miss Abbott."

"At the library?" Elizabeth Anne asked.

"That's right. She can help us find the information we need."

Hiram drove them to the library. They pulled into a parking space in front of the low, white-boarded building. Jimmy lost some of his enthusiasm when he saw three bikes in the bike rack near the hedge. One had a red flag just like the flag on the back of Buck's bike.

"The last person I want to see," Jimmy whispered. "What else is going to go wrong?" He hung back, entering after the others.

Buck and his friends were sprawled in chairs in the nonfiction room. They grinned when they saw Jimmy and Hiram. Jimmy stiffened and went to stand beside Hiram.

Miss Abbott quickly found the books they needed. She hovered over them as Gran gave each person several books to search through.

"Am I right in supposing this is no ordinary visit?" Miss Abbott asked.

"You certainly are, Martha," Granny said. "That sea creature everyone is in such a flap about has turned out to be a manatee."

Jimmy didn't have to look around to know that the three boys were listening. He could practically feel their eyes boring a hole in his back.

"I just knew it would be something like that!" Miss Abbott's lips pursed. "Monster indeed! How stories get started!"

Jimmy felt his cheeks redden. He turned the pages of the book rapidly. He didn't look up.

"Yes, isn't it something?" Granny said calmly. "What do you have there, Jimmy?"

Jimmy had stopped at a section about manatees. "It says manatees don't hurt people. See, Gran?"

Elizabeth Anne added, "This book says they are between eight and fifteen feet long, and they can weigh up to fifteen hundred pounds. That's big!"

Paul leaned over Jimmy's shoulder. "I was right about people hunting them for their hides and oil. See?"

"Oh, and we used to eat them too," Miss Abbott said quickly.

The three children stared at her. "Eat them?" said Jimmy.

"Oh, of course," she said cheerfully. "They taste rather like pork. My folks lived upriver, and Papa occasionally killed a manatee. But they're protected now. I haven't had manatee for years and years."

Jimmy felt a little sick. He didn't even care that Buck and his friends had joined them. They were thumbing through the book Elizabeth Anne had put down. Hiram changed the subject. "I've heard about manatees being found much farther inland. How do they manage so far from the sea?''

"Oh, my," Miss Abbott said. "They don't live in the sea. They live in coastal areas and even follow the rivers inland for a long way. That is, if the river is wide enough and deep enough.''

Paul straightened up suddenly. "Then Jimmy's manatee isn't coming in from the sea and going back out. She's staying right around here —or going upriver!''

"Then why haven't the hunters found her?'' Elizabeth Anne asked.

Hiram rubbed his chin. "You know, if you saw this area from a plane, it would look like a spider's web of waterways. And for a coastal area, there really aren't many people living around here.''

"I'd say you're right," Miss Abbott agreed. "She has plenty of places to go. And she can stay underwater for twenty to thirty minutes at a time.''

"But why did she let Jimmy see her?" Elizabeth Anne asked.

"This book has a picture of a diver petting a manatee," Jimmy said. "It doesn't look afraid of the diver."

"And it says here that they usually aren't afraid of people," Buck said, looking over Jimmy's shoulder. "But they are often injured by the propellers of motorboats."

"Maybe that's your answer," Hiram said. "She has been hit by a boat before. Remember the scar on her back? She might go into deeper water when she hears the motor of a boat. Then again, she hasn't been here long."

"You mean her chances of being discovered are greater every minute," Gran said. "I think we'd better move along, Miss Abbott. Our time seems to be running out."

Miss Abbott watched them as they put the books away. "What are you going to do?" she asked.

"Get the news to everyone as fast as we can," Gran said. "That means the newspaper and the radio station. By evening, most people should know they've been making a fuss over nothing at all."

"I don't know if they'll thank you for the information," Miss Abbott warned. "Island folk can be a mite touchy."

"Touchy?" Jimmy glanced at Buck to see if he knew what she meant.

"Come on, Jimmy." Elizabeth Anne hurried him out. "I'll explain in the car."

"We can help," Buck said.

Jimmy stopped and stared. "You?"

"Sure," Buck replied. "We know one of the announcers at the radio station. We can ride over there and clue him in."

"Thanks, son," Hiram said. "That would be just fine."

The three boys were on their way before Hiram backed out of the parking lot.

Their car arrived at the newspaper station just as the young reporter drove away. Hiram parked in the place he had left empty. "What now?" he asked.

"Let's talk to the editor," she said.

Inside, the editor got up to greet them. "Mrs. Thompson!" he exclaimed. "Come in. You aren't collecting for the fifteenth annual relief fund for overworked and underpaid anteaters, are you?"

The children grinned and shook their heads.

"That's better," he said cheerfully. "When you came through the door, you looked as solemn as a turkey on the day before Thanksgiving."

"Well, we do have something along that line to discuss," Gran said. "Could we talk?"

"Of course. Have a seat," he replied.

Twenty minutes later, assured of his cooperation, they were on their way home. They passed Buck and the other two boys on the way. Buck gave them a victory sign. Jimmy felt sure that by nightfall, the entire coastal area would know that his monster was a harmless manatee.

Chapter Eleven
A Daring Rescue

"You know something?" Hiram asked as he parked the car. He sat drumming his fingers on the steering wheel.

Gran gathered up her purse and gloves. "What?"

"I've been thinking about that reporter. He sure was in a hurry when he left the office. I was just wondering what news in this area would cause so much excitement?"

Paul groaned. "The manatee!"

"I think she has been sighted," Hiram said. "I just don't know where."

"What can we do?" Jimmy asked anxiously.

"Well, she has to be in the water," Hiram said. "And if she's been located, there'll be a lot of sightseers. Why don't I take the boat out and cruise a while?"

"Can we go too, Gran? Can we?" Jimmy didn't want to be left behind.

"Well, all right," Gran said slowly. "But be careful, Hiram. I don't want the children hurt."

"Yes, ma'am," Hiram said.

"And I'm calling that game warden again," Gran said. "I'll tell him to look out for you."

Hiram nodded. He and the children headed for the boathouse. Blackie raced at their heels.

"Come on, Blackie," Jimmy yelled. "Let's go!" The children struggled into life jackets as Hiram loosened the mooring rope to the *Westwind*. Blackie braced himself on the deck next to Jimmy. The motor growled, then settled into a rumbling roar. Hiram put the gears into reverse. The propellers churned as he backed away from the dock. The boat swung out with the current. Hiram revved the motor. The boat settled against the water and surged forward.

Jimmy leaned into the wind and shouted, ''Which way are we going?''

''Across to the mainland,'' Hiram called back. ''She's more likely to have been spotted from there. Maybe upriver some.''

On the other side of the river he slowed the boat. They cruised along the shoreline, but saw nothing that looked like the manatee.

''This is going to be like looking for a needle in a haystack,'' Hiram said. ''Look for that reporter's car, kids. He probably parked somewhere along the shore.''

He handed Paul a pair of binoculars. Jimmy looked at them enviously. ''See anything?'' he asked. ''Can I have a turn?''

''In a minute,'' Paul replied. He scanned the coastline slowly. ''What are all those kids doing?''

"What kids?" Jimmy turned and looked at the road that ran along the bay. A long line of bikers straggled along the road, heading toward the bridge. The first one had a tall red flag attached to the back of the seat. "It's Buck! And a lot of other kids!"

"They're looking for her too!" Paul trained the binoculars on them. "Buck's pointing in the direction of Baymont Pier."

Hiram swung the boat around and gunned the motor. Jimmy leaned forward. "What's going on?"

"There it is! There's the reporter's car!" Paul yelled.

"Where? Where?"

"Settle down, Jimmy," Hiram said as Paul pointed toward the pier. "Hang on."

He pulled out the throttle, and the boat leaped through the water. As he approached the bridge, he eased up on the throttle. The reporter's car was parked on the riverbank, just down from the pier. Hiram cruised along the bank.

"I see him!" Jimmy shouted. "There!"

The reporter was out on the pier, in front of a crowd of people. He was using his telephoto lens to capture the action that was taking place in the middle of the river. About a half dozen boats were circling in the water. Occasionally one would take a run across the circle, planing out of the water.

Hiram frowned and cut the motor. "Speedboats! Too much horsepower for match sticks like those!"

"Why do you call them match sticks, Hiram?" Jimmy watched the stunts in admiration.

"They have souped up engines for racing," Hiram said. "Too much power for lightweight boats. Well, I guessed wrong, kids. Looks like he's doing a boat show."

"It's not a boat show, Hiram," Paul said. "Look!"

He handed the binoculars to Hiram.

"What is it? What is it?" Jimmy bounced in impatience.

"They're running the manatee," Hiram said grimly. "They're trying to work her to shore."

"What are they going to do?" Elizabeth Anne asked.

"I'm not sure," Hiram replied. He scanned the crowd on the pier. "A pickup truck just pulled up. Three men are running onto the pier with rifles." He put down the binoculars. "That's not good. Let's go!"

"They've got guns," Jimmy wailed.

"It doesn't matter much," Hiram shouted, making the engine roar. "If those boats hit the manatee with their propellers, she'll be in bad shape anyway. Let's get her!"

"Go, Hiram," Paul yelled.

Spray stung their faces as Hiram pushed the big boat as fast as it would go. He swung around the cluster of speedboats, rocking them with his wake.

"Hey, get out of here," the men shouted, shaking their fists at him.

Hiram's answer was to cut in closer, almost swamping one boat with the backwash from his passing.

"Move out!" Hiram shouted. "Move away from the manatee!"

The children weren't sure the men heard Hiram, but there was no mistaking the message in his actions. He circled them again and the cluster broke apart. The third sweep left the men struggling with their boats. The circle was empty.

"She's gone, Hiram," Paul shouted, tapping Hiram on the shoulder. "Look!"

The manatee had made her move. She had shepherded her baby upriver.

"She's not safe yet," Hiram said. "You're not the only one who saw!"

He pointed to a fishing boat that had pulled away from the dock. It headed after the manatee. The baby slowed the sea cow's pace so much that the boat easily closed the gap between them.

"Hiram!" Elizabeth Anne squealed as one man raised his rifle.

"Get down and hold on," Hiram ordered.

The children crouched down in the boat. Jimmy clutched Blackie as the prow cut through the water. They couldn't see what was happening, but they could hear.

Hiram pulled the boat alongside the fishing craft. "Bert Lawson! Hank!" he shouted. "Put that gun down! She's a manatee!"

The bearded man with the rifle lowered it. Both boats slowed as they approached the dark shape in the water. They had her in full view for a moment. Then she and the baby dove. Hiram cut his engine. So did the fishermen.

"A manatee?" Bert called to Hiram. "That big?"

"She's the biggest I've ever seen," Hiram replied. "But she's a manatee, all right."

"Yeah," the man at the wheel said. "I got a good look at her."

"She's got a baby," Jimmy called.

Bert rubbed his beard and made a face. "Oh, boy," he growled. "This tale'll be making the rounds for years."

"Better a foolish tale than a night in jail," Hiram said. He waved at an approaching boat. "Here's the game warden."

The game warden's boat slowed and swung wide as it passed the surfacing manatee. The warden cut the engine and drifted alongside the other boats.

"Got the message," he said. "What's been going on down here?"

"Where have you been, James Purcell?" Hiram scowled. "The only time you're right handy is when the bluefish are running!"

"Upriver at the bird sanctuary," the warden grinned. "And if you didn't drool at bluefish out of season, you wouldn't have any problem with that. What's this manatee doing way down here?"

Jimmy looked across at the other boat. There wasn't a rifle to be seen. He opened his mouth to speak, but Paul dug an elbow into his ribs.

"We are trying to find that out," Hiram said dryly. "She's caused a bit of damage down here. How'll we get her back where she belongs?"

"Just what you're doing," the warden said. "She's on her way. If we spread out and follow along a while, she'll go along. But Hiram . . . I'll talk to you at Land's End tonight!"

Hiram waved at him over the roar of the engines. The boats moved slowly after the sea cow and her calf, edging her gently upriver.

"She'll be safe now, right, Hiram?" Jimmy asked.

"Well, she'll be in safer waters," Hiram answered. "The rest of it is out of our hands."

Chapter Twelve
Land's End

They followed the manatee upriver until it was too dark to see her. The boats returned under running lights. It was a tired crew that reached the dock at Land's End. The warden moored his boat on the other side of the dock and climbed out wearily.

"It's been a long day," he said, stretching. "First the vandalism at the sanctuary, then this. I'm ready for your granny's home cooking."

Granny met them at the door. "Thank the Lord," she said shakily. "I've been so worried about you."

"We got her upriver, ma'am," the game warden said. "She'll head for Blue Cove as fast as she can."

"Blue Cove?" Jimmy asked.

"That's Caleb Wert's place. He has around two hundred acres of land up there. If you can call that water-soaked property real land. But it suits Caleb."

"Why is she going there?" Jimmy persisted.

"After supper, young man," Granny interrupted. "You can ask all the questions you want after everyone has eaten. Right now it's enough to know that the manatee is safe. And all of you are safe."

The pot of stew had simmered on the back of the stove for hours. Granny brought out a platter of fresh bread and put tea on the table. Even Jimmy didn't say anything else until his bowl was empty.

"Leave the dishes until later," Granny told Elizabeth Anne. "Let's go out to the porch to talk."

Jimmy flipped the porch light on. They stretched out in Granny's wicker chairs and enjoyed the night air. James Purcell eased off his boots with a sigh of relief.

"Well, start talking," he told Hiram. "And don't make this one of your famous tales."

Hiram sniffed. "I have plenty of witnesses, James Purcell. Jimmy here was out a mite late one night. He saw the manatee and didn't know what it was. Somehow the tale got out that he saw a monster."

"It was my fault," Jimmy confessed. "When Buck laughed at my monster story, I added some extra details." He turned to Granny. "I'm sorry, Gran. I let my tongue get away with me again."

"Then when the newspaper reporter picked up on the story, Jimmy tried to get it right," Elizabeth Anne said. "But the reporter liked the monster story best."

"Uh-huh," the game warden said. "The new one? Young fellow with a sawed-off mustache?"

"That's the one," Hiram replied. "Now, who's telling this?"

The children sat back in their chairs and grinned. "You are, Hiram," said Jimmy.

"Well, they called it a monster after some damage was done to the fishermen's nets and one of those fancy floating docks was destroyed," Hiram went on. "The island folk got a mite nervous, and business fell off at the cannery."

The game warden laughed. "How did Mr. Flint take that?"

"Not too well," Hiram replied. "He offered a reward of one thousand dollars to anyone who killed the creature responsible for the damage."

"Reward?" The game warden sat up quickly. "No wonder the place was in an uproar when I got back. Dangling one thousand dollars around folks who've had a bad year at fishing is like baiting a bull."

"Some of them took the bait," Hiram continued. "And they started hunting for the monster."

"Had they seen it? These are island folk. They've seen manatees. Why, they'd even recognize the description of one." The warden sounded surprised.

"Uh, the description got changed somewhat," said Hiram. Jimmy looked down at his feet. To his relief, Hiram kept talking. "And they never got a good look at it until this afternoon."

"I see."

"It was the money that sparked the fuse," Hiram continued. "When we tried to get Mr. Flint to back down, he wouldn't. But he changed his reward—said it would be for just capturing the manatee after we told him what it was."

"Are you going to arrest him?" Elizabeth Anne asked eagerly.

James Purcell shook his head. "He did change the reward to capture? Then there's no law against what he did. I don't approve of it and I'll talk to him. But I doubt if it'll do much to change Mr. Flint's character."

"What about the fishermen who were going to shoot it?" Paul asked indignantly. "Shouldn't something be done to them?"

"Did they shoot it?" the game warden asked.

Paul shook his head. "They stopped when they saw it was a manatee."

"That lets them off the hook then."

"What about the speedboaters?" Jimmy asked. "They were trying to hurt her."

"Do you know that for sure? Did they?" James Purcell pulled out his notebook. "Was it that club up by Baymont Pier?"

Jimmy nodded. "They didn't hurt her, but they could have. She's got a long scar that Hiram said might have come from a propeller."

"I've been warning them about recklessness. I'll see to it," the warden said. "But old Caleb put that scar there. He ran over her when she was young. Felt so bad about it that he hauled her to his camp and fixed her up. She's almost like a pet now. She hangs around his cove most of the time.'' He scratched his head. ''I don't know why she's this far downriver.''

''The baby,'' Granny said. ''Little Jimmy. She probably chased him all the way here. He's a lively little thing. In trouble most of the time, I expect.''

The warden snapped his notebook shut and laughed. ''Probably so. Little Jimmy, huh?''

Jimmy ducked his head. ''I'm not always in trouble,'' he mumbled.

Elizabeth Anne and Paul hooted. ''No, not likely.''

Jimmy hesitated. ''Well, I'll be careful what I tell other people from now on,'' he promised. ''Gran, I really promise.''

Granny nodded. ''Remember, children, there is a difference between facts and a good tale.''

''Now Hiram here,'' James Purcell said, grinning, ''he does tell a good tale.''

''He sure does,'' exclaimed Paul and Elizabeth Anne.

But Jimmy was still thinking about the manatee—and Buck. God had sure answered his prayer about Buck. He spoke up. "You know, Buck and his friends turned out to be a big help, after all. They're not as bad as I thought."

"Maybe we should get to know them a little better," said Paul.

"Sounds like a good idea to me," Granny said, smiling at Jimmy. "Why not invite Buck and his friends over Saturday? You come too James. It's time Hiram practiced his grilling."

James Purcell put on his boots and got up. "Thank you, Mrs. Thompson. That sounds great. I've a few things to straighten out in the morning. I'd best be on my way."

They saw him off, then settled back down in the wicker chairs. Hiram's eyes took on a faraway look. "You know," he said, "this whole thing reminds me of—"

He grinned at Gran. "—of a tale about Old Blackjack—"

Granny smiled back at him, and Hiram continued. His voice rose and he wiggled his eyebrows
as the children gathered around. "It was a hot,
wet day, so sticky that even the mosquitos
couldn't rev up their wings for a takeoff. . . ."